WE DEDICATE THIS BOOK TO OUR LITTLE YOUNG BUCKS:
KOURTNEY, ZACHARY, ALISON AND GREGORY
-MJ & -NJ

TO ZACHARY JAMES, MY NUMBER ONE WRESTLING BUDDY
- DC

PUBLISHED BY TRISM BOOKS, DEERFIELD, IL, USA

THE ELITE TEAM: YOUNG BUCKS STAND TALL

TEXT COPYRIGHT © 2018 BY MATT JACKSON; NICK JACKSON
ILLUSTRATIONS COPYRIGHT © 2018 BY DYLAN COBURN

THE ELITE TEAM: YOUNG BUCKS STAND TALL/WRITTEN BY MATT JACKSON; NICK JACKSON; ILLUSTRATED BY DYLAN COBURN

ISBN 978-0-9888338-8-3

1. WRESTLING - JUVENILE LITERATURE 2. SELF ESTEEM - JUVENILE LITERATURE 3. FRIENDSHIP - JUVENILE LITERATURE
4. BULLYING - JUVENILE LITERATURE I.TITLE.
THE ARTWORK WAS CREATED DIGITALLY
BOOK DESIGN BY ERICA WEISZ; EDITED BY SAM WEISZ
PRINTED IN MALAYSIA

10 9 8 7 6 5 4 3 2 1
WWW.TRISMBOOKS.COM

THE ELITE TEAM
YOUNG BUCKS
STAND TALL

STORY BY
MATT AND NICK JACKSON

ILLUSTRATIONS BY
DYLAN COBURN

TRISM BOOKS
TURNING PAGES. GROWING MINDS.

MATT AND NICK WERE INSEPARABLE.

THEY WENT TO SCHOOL TOGETHER,

ONE DAY AT SCHOOL, *MATT*, *NICK* AND *THE ELITE TEAM* WERE PRACTICING DURING *RECESS*...

MARTY SANG, "*I WANT TO BE A POP STAR!*"

ADAM LASSOED, "*I WANT TO BE A COWBOY!*" *CODY* OF COURSE WANTED TO BE THE *PRESIDENT.*

AND *KENNY* A *JANITOR.*

SNOOPING NEARBY, *JIMMY* JUST *CROSSED* HIS ARMS AND *ROLLED* HIS EYES.

AS *JIMMY* GOT UP FROM THE GROUND, *MATT* AND *NICK* LOOKED UP. *WAY UP*.

SAD, THEY **RACED** HOME TOGETHER...

FLUNG THE DOOR OPEN TOGETHER...

AND **FLOPPED** ONTO THE RUG TOGETHER.

THEY **HAD** TO FIGURE OUT A WAY TO **GET BIG!**

FOR **DINNER** THEY PILED THEIR PLATES **EXTRA TALL** WITH **BROCCOLI** AND **SPINACH**.

MATT AND NICK MADE EVERY ATTEMPT TO GROW...

WITHOUT ANY SUCCESS.

FINALLY, DURING BEDTIME PRAYERS, *THEY ASKED TO BE BIGGER.*

BACK AT SCHOOL, **MATT** AND **NICK** STILL FELT **SMALL.**

AT RECESS, THEY **DODGED** THEIR **WRESTLING PRACTICE** AND SKIPPED **THE ELITE TEAM** CLUB MEETING.

THEY EVEN **STOPPED** WEARING **MATCHING GEAR.**

THEY CONTINUED TO *MOPE* AROUND THE HOUSE UNTIL THEIR *DAD* SURPRISED THEM WITH *WRESTLING TICKETS* FOR THE *BIG EVENT.*

HE *WRAPPED* THEIR MATCHING *ZEBRA HEADBANDS* THROUGH THEIR HAIR AS THEY RELUCTANTLY MADE SIGNS.

THEN HE *DRAGGED* THEM TO THE *ARENA.*

MATT HEARD THE CROWD'S CHEERS. NICK SAW THE FANS' SIGNS.

THE *LIGHTS* FADED. THE *MUSIC* CAME ON.

THE *CROWD ROARED* FOR THE FIRST *WRESTLER* AS HE APPROACHED THE RING.

MATT AND NICK WATCHED IN AMAZEMENT AS THE WRESTLER, SAMSON THE SPECTACULAR, DARTED, FLIPPED, AND ROLLED AROUND THE RING.

WHUMP!

"1...2....3!"
COUNTED THE REF.

THEIR PRAYERS WERE ANSWERED. MATT AND NICK *FELT BIGGER* FROM THEIR EXPERIENCE AT THE WRESTLING MATCH. THEY WERE *DETERMINED* TO MAKE A COMEBACK.

THEY CALLED AN EMERGENCY *ELITE TEAM CLUB MEETING* FOR RECESS THE NEXT DAY.

THE ELITES WERE *EXCITED* TO HEAR THEIR VOICES AGAIN.

JIMMY PUFFED UP HIS CHEST, AND LOOKED THEM SQUARE IN THE EYE.

YOU LITTLE RUNTS WOULD GET EATEN ALIVE IN THE RING.

MATT AND NICK STOOD TALL.

THE ELITE TEAM REALIZED THEIR FRIENDS, THE YOUNG BUCKS, NEEDED THEM.

MARTY STOOD UP IN DEFENSE.

ADAM FOLLOWED.

CODY STOOD UP AND CHEERED...

MATT'S **FASTER** THAN THE FASTEST **CHEETAH!**

KENNY CHIMED IN...

AND NICK CAN **FLY** HIGHER THAN A **HAWK!**

THE YOUNG BUCKS MADE IT THEIR MISSION TO HELP OTHERS STAND UP TO ALL THE JIMMYS OUT THERE.